A Note from Michelle about *The Big Turkey Escape*

Hi! I'm Michelle Tanner. I'm nine years And I'm spending my Thanksgiving on a farm. Cool, right?

Wrong! Because my new best friend—Tom the turkey—is on the dinner menu! I have to come up with a plan to save him. I just have to.

No one in my whole family understands how I feel about Tom—and I have a *very* big family. There's my dad and my two older sisters, D.J. and Stephanie. But that's not all.

My mom died when I was little. So my uncle Jesse moved in to help Dad take care of us. So did Joey Gladstone. He's my dad's friend from college. It's almost like having three dads. But that's still not all!

First Uncle Jesse got married to Becky Donaldson. Then they had twin boys, Nicky and Alex. The twins are four years old now. And they're so cute.

That's nine people. Our dog, Comet, makes ten. Sure it gets kind of crazy sometimes. But I wouldn't change it for anything. It's so much fun living in a full house!

FULL HOUSE™ MICHELLE novels

Available from MINSTREL Books

FULL HOUSE™
Michelle

The Big Turkey Escape

Jean Waricha

A Parachute Press Book

Published by POCKET BOOKS
New York   London   Toronto   Sydney   Tokyo   Singapore

This book is a work of fiction. Names, characters, places and inci-
dents are products of the author's imagination or are used ficti-
tiously. Any resemblance to actual events or locales or persons,
living or dead, is entirely coincidental.

A MINSTREL PAPERBACK *Original*

A Minstrel Book published by
POCKET BOOKS, a division of Simon & Schuster Inc.
1230 Avenue of the Americas, New York, NY 10020

A PARACHUTE PRESS BOOK

READING Copyright © and ™ 1996 by Warner Bros.

FULL HOUSE, characters, names and all related indicia are
trademarks of Warner Bros. © 1996.

All rights reserved, including the right to reproduce
this book or portions thereof in any form whatsoever.
For information address Pocket Books, 1230 Avenue
of the Americas, New York, NY 10020

ISBN: 0-671-56836-1

First Minstrel Books printing November 1996

10 9 8 7 6 5 4 3 2 1

A MINSTREL BOOK and colophon are registered trademarks of
Simon & Schuster Inc.

Cover photo by Schultz Photography

Printed in the U.S.A.

The Big Turkey Escape

Chapter

1

❤ "Over the river and through the woods, to Aunt Becky's friend's house we go," Michelle Tanner bellowed.

Michelle and her family were on their way to Oregon for Thanksgiving. All nine of them were crammed into the van they rented for the trip.

"The van knows the way—" Michelle continued.

"Stop!" Michelle's eighteen-year-old sister, D.J., ordered. "Stop right now! You've sung that song about twenty times since we left San Francisco."

"Stephanie likes this song," Michelle protested. She turned to her thirteen-year-old sister. "Right?"

Stephanie didn't answer. She kept bobbing her head to some song on her Walkman.

Michelle twisted around in her seat and gave her uncle Jesse a big smile. Jesse would want her to keep singing. He loved music. "You like this song, don't you?" she asked.

"Uh, sure," Jesse answered. "But the twins just fell asleep. Maybe you should stop for a while."

Michelle sighed. The puff of air blew up the bangs of her long, strawberry-blond hair. She glanced at the four-year-old boys. They looked so nice and comfy in their car seats.

I bet Nicky and Alex will sleep for hours, Michelle thought. And I want to sing now.

Joey Gladstone sat on the other side of the twins, fast asleep too. His snoring is louder than my singing, Michelle thought. But no one is telling *him* to be quiet.

Joey was her father's friend from college. He lived with them. And Uncle Jesse and Aunt Becky and the twins lived on the third floor. It was a *very* full house! And now they were all taking a trip together.

Too bad Comet couldn't come, Michelle thought. The Tanners' golden retriever was too big to squeeze into the van, so he was spending Thanksgiving at Michelle's best friend Cassie's house.

Michelle turned around so she could talk to her dad and Aunt Becky in the front seat. "I can't wait to get to the Andersons' farm, Aunt Becky. Cassie and Mandy are so jealous—especially because I get to take the whole week off from school."

"There is a lot you can learn on a farm," Danny Tanner told Michelle. "Maybe you can give Mrs. Yoshida and the class a report when we get back."

"Will there be cows on the farm?" Michelle asked her dad.

3

"Yes," Danny replied.

"How about horses?" Michelle asked.

"Lots of horses!" Danny said.

"Pigs?"

"Oh, I'm sure there will be a few pigs," her dad answered.

"What about chickens?"

"Definitely."

"How about rabbits?"

Michelle heard D.J. groan behind her, but she ignored her sister.

"Probably," Danny said.

"Any sheep?"

"Yes!"

"Goats?"

"Yes! Yes, Michelle! Yes! Yes! Yes!"

"How about kangaroos?"

"Yes!" Danny exclaimed.

Jesse, D.J., and Aunt Becky laughed. Michelle cracked up. "Gotcha, Dad!"

"You tricked me!" Danny cried. He tried

to sound upset, but Michelle could tell he thought her joke was funny too.

"Hey, look!" Michelle shouted. "There's a sign for a petting zoo! Can we stop?"

"No," Danny said. "When we get to the farm you can pet all the animals you want."

"How much longer?" Michelle asked. "We've been in the car about a gazillion hours already."

When they left home the sun wasn't even up, and now it was dark. Sure, they stopped for lunch—but Michelle couldn't stand being in the car one more second.

"We're almost there," Aunt Becky told her. "I remember that petting zoo sign from the last time I was here. I took the bus, and the zoo was the stop right before the farm. We're only a couple of miles away."

Michelle bounced up and down on her seat. Finally!

"Turn left up there," Aunt Becky said.

Danny swung the van onto a narrow dirt road.

They drove down the road for a few minutes. Michelle gazed out the window at acres and acres of farmland. Cool, she thought. We really are out in the country!

"We're here!" Aunt Becky cried. "I can see Maria and Sam on the porch!" Aunt Becky pointed up ahead to a big white farmhouse.

Danny parked the van in front of the house. Michelle could see a light shining on a red barn farther away. This is going to be so much fun, she thought. A real farm with a barn and everything.

Michelle poked Stephanie. "Come on! Let's get out!"

Stephanie pulled off her Walkman and climbed out of the van. D.J. and Michelle followed right behind her. Then Jesse and Joey piled out. They each carried one of the twins, who were both still asleep.

A short woman with curly brown hair ran up to Aunt Becky and gave her a big hug. A skinny man in jeans and a blue shirt kissed her on the cheek.

"Everybody," Aunt Becky called. "This is Sam and Maria. I've known Maria since I was Michelle's age! We went to grade school together."

Whoa! Michelle thought. Maybe someday I'll be visiting Cassie or Mandy for Thanksgiving. It was weird to think of either of her two best friends living in a different state—and hardly ever seeing them.

"You two go in the house and catch up on things," Sam said to Maria and Aunt Becky. "I'll help everyone get settled."

Aunt Becky and Maria headed inside, talking and laughing. Danny opened the van's back door and started unloading the suitcases.

Hssss! Hssss!

Michelle spun around.

And saw a huge goose headed toward her. It stretched its wings straight out. It opened its sharp beak wide.

Michelle couldn't stop staring at the inside of the goose's mouth.

Hssss! The goose snapped its beak at Michelle.

And then it lunged at her!

"*Helllp!* It's going to bite me!" she screeched.

Hsss! Hsss!

Michelle tried to run away. But the goose ran faster. She felt her tennis shoe slide across a patch of mud. She waved her arms, trying to catch her balance.

Too late.

Splat!

Michelle plopped down in a gooey puddle of mud!

Chapter
2

♥ Sam rushed up and shooed away the goose.

"Are you okay?" Danny asked. He ran over and helped Michelle to her feet.

"I think so," she answered. Mud covered her hands. It soaked through her light blue sweater. It dripped down the legs of her jeans.

"Come on!" D.J. tugged Michelle into the house. "I'll help you clean up."

Michelle washed off the mud and changed her clothes. Then everyone sat down around the big wooden kitchen table for a bite to eat. Michelle liked the flowered cushions tied to the chairs and the matching curtains.

"Michelle, you sure made a big splash out there!" Jesse joked.

"Yes, you did, you silly *goose!*" Joey added.

D.J. groaned. "That's so lame, Joey."

Michelle felt glad when everyone started teasing Joey about his bad jokes. She didn't want to hear another word about how funny she looked covered in mud.

When they finished eating, Maria showed the girls to their room. She told them it was where her nieces stay when they come to visit. It was huge, with three beds and three dressers. The beds were covered with beautiful flowered quilts, and on the floor was a colorful rug with a picture of a farmhouse woven into it.

"I think it's going to be a great week," Stephanie said. "Don't you, Michelle?" She snapped off the light and crawled into the bed next to Michelle's.

"Yeah, sure," Michelle grumbled. She snuggled down under the flowered quilt. "My first day on the farm and I get attacked by a goose!"

D.J. snorted.

"It's not funny!" Michelle cried. She sat up and threw her pillow at D.J. It didn't go far enough—it hit Stephanie instead.

Stephanie threw the pillow back at Michelle. "Go to sleep. I'm sure we'll find something fun to do tomorrow."

I just hope the rest of the animals on this farm aren't as mean as that goose! Michelle thought as she drifted off to sleep.

Michelle woke up with her heart pounding. What was that sound?

She listened closely.

There it was again.

A rustling sound.

11

Is something in the room with us? It was too dark to tell.

"Stephanie? D.J.?" she called softly. "Is that you?"

No answer.

Then something bumped against the door.

Okay, Michelle told herself. Whatever it is is *outside* our bedroom.

She heard another bump. But it's trying to get *in!*

Michelle wanted to wake her sisters. But they would call her a baby if she did.

Michelle quickly got dressed. Then she peeked into the hallway. Nothing there.

But she thought she saw something darting down the stairs. Something with feathers. Michelle hesitated for a minute—then she hurried down the stairs after it. She had to find out what it was.

"Michelle! What are you doing up so early?"

Michelle turned and saw Maria standing

12

in the kitchen doorway. "Did you see it?" she cried.

"See what?" Maria asked.

"I don't know," Michelle answered. "Some kind of animal, I think. It was trying to get into our room, and I followed it down here."

"You must have been dreaming," Maria said. "Sometimes I have dreams so real, I'm sure they really happened. Sam always laughs at me."

"No!" Michelle exclaimed. "I know I heard something. Listen!"

Michelle and Maria stood very still, listening hard. Nothing.

"Why don't you lie down on the couch," Maria suggested. She led the way into the living room. "It's too early for you to be up."

Michelle curled up on the couch. Maybe I *was* dreaming, she thought.

"I'll be right back with a blanket," Maria said.

As soon as Maria left the room, Michelle heard another sound behind the couch. *Scratch! Scratch! Scratch!*

Oh, no! It's in here with me!

Scratch! Scratch! Scratch!

And it has claws!

Michelle opened her mouth to scream for Maria—then she snapped it shut again. If I yell, the animal will know I'm here, she thought. And then it will come after me.

Michelle waited. Trying not to move. Trying not to breathe too loud.

No rustling sound. No scratching.

Maybe it's gone. I'll just take a tiny peek, Michelle thought. She inched her way up until she could see over the back of the couch.

A pair of the meanest eyes she had ever seen glared back at her!

"Maria!" Michelle screamed. "It's in here!"

Maria ran into the living room. "Hey! You

were right, Michelle. I should have known. That turkey is always sneaking into the house!" she exclaimed.

Turkey? Michelle sat all the way up and stared at the creature. Yep, it was a turkey all right.

Maria snapped open the blanket. She flapped it at the turkey. "Shoo!" she cried. "Shoo!"

Michelle followed Maria as she herded the big turkey through the kitchen and out the door.

"Can I stay up with you?" Michelle asked. "I don't think I can fall back asleep now."

"Sure," Maria said. "You can help me make breakfast. I have a special job for you. I bet it's something you'll like."

Maria pulled a large basket down from the kitchen cabinet and handed it to Michelle. "Take this over to the barn and collect some fresh eggs."

"That sounds like fun! Where are they?" Michelle asked. "How many should I get?"

"They're easy to find," Maria said. "They are right in the chicken boxes. Bring back about two dozen."

Maria pulled a sweatshirt and a wool hat out of the kitchen closet. "Put these on. It's cold out there."

Michelle slipped them on and headed out the door. "I'll be right back with the eggs," she called.

The cold air stung Michelle's fingers and nose as she raced toward the barn. She passed a bright green tractor. Its tires were huge! I bet it would be fun to ride sitting up so high, she thought.

She struggled to open the big barn door, then slammed it shut behind her.

It sure smells funny in here, she thought, sniffing the air. She gazed around the barn, searching for the chickens. "Ah-ha! There they are," she said, spotting them at the far end of the barn.

Michelle began to walk toward the chickens. She slowly made her way between two rows of cows to get there. She studied the animals as she walked. They were huge. I bet they could smash down their stalls with their hooves, Michelle thought.

But most of the cows had their eyes closed. They are probably still asleep, she thought. Nothing to worry about.

Michelle took a deep breath and hurried across the barn. None of the cows even mooed at her.

So far, so good, she thought.

Michelle studied the chickens. There were about fifteen of them, and each sat on a nest of straw resting in a wooden box. The wooden boxes were lined up on shelves. It was like looking at a cupboard full of chickens! But they weren't the cute, fuzzy little chicks Michelle had seen in the pet stores at

Easter time. These chickens were big—with sharp beaks.

Well, at least they're smaller than the goose and the turkey, Michelle thought.

She crept up to the closest chicken. It was brown and red with little black eyes. Mean little black eyes.

I guess I just have to stick my hand in and get the eggs. "Nice chicken! Nice, nice chicken!"

Michelle set down her basket. She slid her fingers past the soft, smooth chicken feathers. The chicken didn't *seem* to mind, but all Michelle could feel was straw.

She inched her fingers in a little farther. She felt something warm, and round, and hard. Eggs! Yes!

Michelle grabbed an egg in each hand. She pulled them out—and knocked the chicken right off its nest.

The chicken flew at Michelle. Its feathers flapped against her face. She couldn't see.

She threw her hands up to protect her eyes. *Splat! Splat!* Both the eggs hit the floor.

The chicken flew back to its shelf—and knocked into another chicken.

Squawk! Squawk! Squawk!

The other chicken flapped its wings wildly, which upset the rest of the chickens.

They all began pecking and squawking and flapping. Hay and feathers filled the air.

One pecked at Michelle's shoe. Another one nipped her fingers.

"Stop it! Stop it!" she cried, trying to edge away.

She backed into the nests and—*splat!* An egg tumbled from one and landed right on her head.

Chapter 3

♥ "Oh, gross!" Michelle cried as the egg yolk ran down her cheek. She wiped off her face with her sleeve and yanked off her slimy hat. She glared at the squawking birds.

These chickens hate me! Just like all the other animals on this farm! I'm getting out of here.

Michelle took two steps toward the front of the barn—and stopped. No, she thought. No way. I'm not letting those chickens win.

Michelle spun around to face them. "I

don't care what you do!" she shouted at the chickens. "I'm getting those eggs!"

She started toward the nests. All right! she thought. The chickens were so busy fighting each other and trying to peck Michelle that all the nests were empty.

Michelle reached for an egg. A yellow and brown hen flapped up to the nest. It grabbed Michelle's little finger in its beak. She didn't care. While the chicken was nibbling on her left hand, she used her right hand to transfer three eggs from the nest to her basket.

Only about twenty more to go, Michelle thought. She shook her left hand until the chicken let go. Then she bent down and emptied another nest. A chicken landed on her back and started pecking her ponytail!

Michelle shook her head and the chicken flapped off, feathers flying. She moved on to the next nest. One of the chickens tried to climb straight up the leg of her jeans. She could feel its little claws scraping her.

"Out of my way, chickens!" Michelle shouted. She grabbed one egg after the other.

Done! Finally!

She noticed a little door underneath the shelves. That must be for the chickens to go in and out. I bet I can use it for a shortcut.

She dropped to her hands and knees and squeezed through. Then she jumped to her feet. I did it! Michelle thought. I got the eggs! Hurray for me! She hurried back to the farmhouse.

"I was just about to send someone out to look for you!" Maria cried when Michelle came through the door.

"What happened to you?" Danny exclaimed.

Michelle glanced down at herself. She was covered with hay and dirt and chicken feathers. She pulled a long yellow feather out of her hair and tried to look cool. "Umm, nothing. I just collected some eggs for breakfast, that's all." She handed the basket to Maria and started to sit down between Stephanie and D.J.

"Unh-unh," her dad said. "Clean clothes first."

D.J. reached up and pulled a brown feather out of Michelle's hair. "Are you sure you were collecting eggs and not feathers?" she asked.

Stephanie plucked a red feather from Michelle's sweatshirt and tickled Michelle's nose with it. Michelle grabbed the feather away from her.

Maria started cracking the eggs into the frying pan. "Would you like me to make some of my special pancakes to go with those?" Danny asked her.

"That would be great," Michelle heard Maria answer as she headed out the door. "My kitchen is your kitchen."

Michelle rushed up to her room, taking the steps two at a time. Dad would go nuts if he had to go a day without cooking, Michelle thought. But she loved his pancakes, so she wasn't complaining.

Michelle changed her clothes as fast as she could. She was starving. She trotted down the stairs and back to her spot at the kitchen table. Aunt Becky and Uncle Jesse wandered into the kitchen after her, each holding one of the twins by the hand.

"Michelle gathered fresh eggs for us for breakfast," Danny announced. He sounded proud of her.

"Good job!" Joey called. He strolled into the kitchen and patted Michelle on the head. "Did you decide to give yourself an egg shampoo while you were at it?" he asked.

Before Michelle could answer, Sam came in from outside with a big basket full of apples. His cheeks were bright red from the cold.

"Just in time to eat," Maria told him. She

and Danny started piling big plates of food on the table.

"Hey, can we have a tour of the farm after breakfast?" D.J. asked.

"Great idea!" Stephanie said. She licked a drop of maple syrup off her bottom lip.

I've seen enough of the farm, Michelle thought. I've been snapped at by a goose, chased by a turkey, and practically pecked to death by a hen house full of chickens.

"What about you, Michelle?" Danny said. "Your own private petting zoo is right outside the door."

"Uhh . . . maybe later. I think I'll help clean up all this breakfast stuff," Michelle said.

"Go!" Joey said. "Your dad already volunteered Jesse and me for cleanup duty. As usual!"

"Umm . . . but Aunt Becky might need help with the twins," Michelle said.

"Don't worry about me," Aunt Becky told

her. "I can handle Nicky and Alex. You enjoy the farm."

Yeah, right, Michelle thought. But what could she do? She couldn't come up with one more excuse.

"Come on! This tour bus is leaving!" Maria called. D.J., Stephanie, Danny, and Maria pulled on sweaters and hats. Michelle followed them out the door and into the barn.

"Here's something you have to see," Maria called. She opened a stall on the right.

"Oh, look at the babies," Stephanie cooed.

Michelle pushed her way forward. Babies didn't sound too scary. She saw two little red calves. One of them had a big white streak down his nose. They *were* pretty cute.

Maria handed Michelle and her sisters some carrots. "Go ahead and feed them," she said.

D.J. and Stephanie each held out carrots

to the calves. "Why don't you feed this one, Michelle?" Maria opened the next stall and led out an enormous red and white cow. She tied it to a post.

The top of Michelle's head barely came to the cow's chin. It chomped on a mouthful of hay, and she could hear its big teeth grinding together.

"That goose you met yesterday is a lot tougher than this old girl," Maria told her. "She won't hurt you. I promise."

Michelle held out the carrot and tried to smile. Maybe just the birds on the farm are mean, she thought. Maybe I can make friends with this cow.

The cow's rough tongue brushed against Michelle's hand. It was twice as big as Comet's tongue—and three times as slimy! She jerked her hand away and the carrot flew to the ground near the cow's hind legs. "Sorry," she muttered.

Michelle hurried over and bent down to get the carrot.

Whap! The cow's smelly old tail smacked her in the face.

Michelle stumbled back—and felt her feet sink down into something squishy. Squishy *and* smelly!

Chapter 4

♥ "Can't we just clean my shoes?" Michelle begged. "Do we really have to throw them away?"

"You know I'm the Master of Clean," her dad said. "But even I can't save those shoes. You were up to your ankles in cow poop."

"Do we have to talk about this at lunch?" D.J. complained. They all sat around the big kitchen table, finishing up their sandwiches.

"But these are my favorite, favorite shoes," Michelle explained. "Mandy and Cassie have a pair just like them. We bought them together. I chose the pink ones, Mandy chose the purple ones, and Cassie chose the yellow ones."

"I'm sorry, but we have to throw them out," Danny said.

"You don't want to walk around smelling like the tail end of a cow, do you?" Joey joked. "People might start calling you Moo-chelle!"

Everyone laughed. Except Michelle.

I hate cows, she thought. I hate cows, and geese, and turkeys, and chickens. I hate farms! I wish we could go home *now*.

"Sam and I are going into town for some supplies," Maria announced. "Who wants to go?"

Town! That meant away from the farm and all the farm animals. Michelle opened her mouth.

But before she could say a word, her dad jumped in. "We're all going to stay here," he said. "I have a little surprise planned for you. It should be ready when you get back."

"Dad, please, can't I—"

"No, Michelle," Danny said firmly. "I need everybody's help for this."

"Okay," Sam said. "We'll see you all later, then."

"I can hardly wait to see the surprise!" Maria cried as they headed out the door.

"So, what *is* the big surprise?" D.J. asked the second the door closed behind the Andersons.

"Are we going to make them an incredible dinner?" Aunt Becky asked.

"No," Danny answered. "Not even close."

"Are we going to make paper turkeys and decorate the house for Thanksgiving?" Michelle asked.

"No," Danny said. "But you're a little bit closer."

"Just tell us!" Stephanie said.

"We're going to clean the barn," Danny

31

explained. "That will be a great surprise for Maria and Sam."

"I think I have to go somewhere," Joey said.

"Me too," D.J. said.

Everyone sprang up from the table and headed in different directions.

"Freeze!" Danny shouted. "No one is going anywhere—except to the barn. I have a job for each of you."

Stephanie groaned.

"The sooner we start—" Danny began.

"The sooner we finish!" everyone yelled.

"Dad must have gotten a cleaning attack," D.J. mumbled as they headed to the barn. "He's gone one whole day without using a vacuum cleaner!"

"Joey, you clean out the horses' stalls," Danny called when they were all in the barn. "D.J. and Stephanie, you two polish all the farm tools. I want those shovels and hoes to sparkle."

Danny handed Aunt Becky and Jesse a big piece of paper with a drawing of the inside of the barn on it. "You've got to be kidding!" Jesse exclaimed as he studied it. "You want us to arrange the horses and cows by size and color?"

"That's right," Danny said. "And follow my color scheme. This barn is going to look incredible when we're through."

"What's my job?" Michelle asked.

"I want you to clean the turkey pen. It's back in that corner," Danny said.

Oh, no! Michelle thought. *Not that horrible turkey!* "Can't I trade with D.J. or Stephanie? That turkey hates me! All the animals on this whole farm hate me!" she cried.

"It's just your imagination." Danny led Michelle back to the pen. "Look at him," Danny said.

The turkey spread his wings and gave a little hop. *Gobble, gobble, gobble.*

Michelle giggled. The turkey was sort of

33

funny. He had a big round body with lots of tail feathers, a pair of skinny legs with bird claws on the ends, and a little head with a sharp beak. A big flap of red skin hung down under his chin. The skin wobbled when he gobbled.

"You'll be fine," Danny told her. "I have to go make blue bows for the boy animals and pink bows for the girls. Yell if you need me."

Michelle opened the gate and stepped into the pen. She latched the gate—then stood absolutely still. The turkey swaggered over to her.

He's going to bite me. I know it, Michelle thought. She squeezed her eyes shut—and felt something soft brush up against her legs.

She opened her eyes. The turkey rubbed against her legs again. He blinked at her with his bright, shiny black eyes.

Hey! I think this turkey likes me! "How could I have thought you had mean eyes?"

Michelle asked. "You're awfully cute. Want to be friends?"

Gobble, gobble, gobble.

That means yes, Michelle decided. "If we're going to be friends, you need a name. How about Tom? You look like a Tom."

"What's going on over there?" Danny called.

"I'm cleaning," Michelle yelled back.

Michelle leaned down until she was nose to beak with the turkey. "No more fooling around, Tom. We've got to clean your pen."

Michelle found a broom. She swept all the old hay out of the pen and replaced it with clean hay. Tom followed her every move.

"You must be hungry after all that cleaning, Tom," Michelle said. "Let's find you something to eat."

Michelle spotted a bin full of corn. Tom ate some right out of her hand. It tickled!

I have to show Dad, she thought. "Come on, Tom," she called. She found Danny inspecting the horses' stalls. He had on a white glove so he could catch every speck of dust.

"Watch this!" Michelle called. Michelle held out a handful of corn and Tom ate it right up. "He likes me!"

She noticed a strange expression on her father's face. "What's wrong?" she asked.

Danny shook his head. "Michelle, we need to have a little talk about you and the turkey. I don't think—"

"They're here!" Joey shouted.

"Wait until they see the barn," D.J. yelled.

"What, Dad?" Michelle asked. "What about Tom? What?"

Chapter 5

Chapter

5

♥ "We'll talk after we give the Andersons their surprise," Danny told Michelle. "I need to explain something to you about the turkey."

"Can we let Sam and Maria in the barn?" Stephanie asked.

Danny trotted up to the barn door. He leaned outside. "Close your eyes and you can come in," he called to them. "I want this to be a complete surprise!"

Stephanie and D.J. guided Sam and Maria inside. Michelle hurried over to them. She

37

wanted to see their faces clearly when they saw how beautiful the barn looked.

"Okay!" Danny yelled. "Open them!"

Sam and Maria opened their eyes. Neither of them said a word. Sam's mouth hung open as he stared at the big bows the animals wore and the super-shiny tools on the walls.

Maria's face turned red—and she started to cough. She covered her mouth with both hands, coughing and coughing. Michelle thought her coughs sounded a lot like laughs.

"We . . . uh . . . we don't know what to say," Maria told Danny. A nanny goat wandered toward them—chomping on her pink bow. Maria had another coughing fit.

Michelle inched up to Stephanie. "Do you think they like their surprise?"

"I don't think so," Stephanie whispered back.

"You did . . . a great job," Sam said

slowly. "But we don't want . . . you to spend your vacation working. Just have fun. From now on the barn is off limits to you, Danny!"

Danny smiled. "Are you sure there is nothing else we can help you with?"

"You can help us unload the car," Maria said.

"We'll all help," Becky answered.

Michelle followed everyone out to the Andersons' station wagon. Tom the turkey followed Michelle.

She helped haul groceries into the house. Every bag held some special treat for their Thanksgiving feast. Cranberries, chestnuts for the stuffing, chocolate cookies for Michelle's favorite icebox cake.

But there was one thing missing. The turkey.

Gobble, gobble, gobble.

Michelle stared at Tom. No, she thought. No way.

She rushed up to the house and opened

the back door—but she didn't step inside. "Do you think we should tell Michelle?" she heard Maria ask.

Michelle felt her stomach lurch.

"Maybe we should wait until Thanksgiving Day," Aunt Becky suggested.

"No, I have to tell her tonight," Danny said. "She'll become more attached to him if we wait."

Michelle wrapped her arms around herself. She shook her head. No, no, no.

They are really going to do it, Michelle thought. They are planning to serve Tom for our Thanksgiving dinner!

Chapter
6

♥ Michelle slammed through the kitchen door. "No! You can't do it!" she cried. "You can't hurt Tom!"

"Oh, Michelle," Maria said. "We didn't mean for you to find out like that."

"Honey, remember I told you we needed to talk about Tom?" Danny asked. "Well—"

"Can't we have something else for Thanksgiving dinner?" Michelle interrupted. "Please, please, please. Tom's my friend."

Sam and Maria glanced at each other. "I'm sorry, Michelle," Sam said. "But—"

Michelle didn't wait for Sam to finish. She pushed past everyone and ran up the stairs to her bedroom. She slammed the door shut behind her.

How could they do that? How could they eat Tom for Thanksgiving dinner?

Michelle heard a knock on the door, then her father stepped inside. He led her over to her bed and they sat down.

"Dad, you can't let them do anything bad to Tom," Michelle begged. "You have to stop them."

Danny placed his arm around her. "I should have told you about Tom before you made friends with him," he said. "You have to understand that this is a farm, Michelle. It's not a petting zoo. The Andersons' job is to raise fruit and vegetables—and animals—for people to eat."

"It's not fair," Michelle said.

"Honey, I know it's hard. But people have to eat—and their food comes from farms

42

like this. Do you understand?" Danny asked.

Michelle nodded. She understood all right. She understood her dad wasn't going to help her save Tom.

So I'll just have to come up with a plan to rescue my new friend all by myself, she thought.

Gobble, gobble, gobble.

"Shhh!" Michelle smoothed the feathers on Tom's back. "I snuck out of the house as soon as I could. I had to wait almost an hour before the coast was clear. I don't want anyone to know I'm in here with you."

Gobble, gobble, gobble.

Michelle had to lead Tom away from the farm—fast. But if he kept making so much noise, they were going to get caught!

She looped a piece of rope around Tom's neck and tied it in a loose knot. "Come on."

Michelle led Tom to the corn bin. She

filled her coat pockets with corn so the turkey would have something to eat. Then she walked him to the little door under the chicken boxes.

"This is my secret shortcut," Michelle whispered. She crouched down and opened the door. She peered out to make sure no one would see them escape.

Michelle crawled through the small door and held it open for Tom. But he wouldn't come out.

Michelle peered over her shoulder. Still no one around. She tugged on the rope. Tom tugged back.

She stuck her head back through the little door. "Tom, I know you can fit. I'm a lot bigger than you are!" Michelle said.

Tom didn't move. Michelle reached through the door and wrapped her arms around the turkey.

She gave Tom a big yank. He popped out

the door—and landed in Michelle's lap! *Gobble, gobble, gobble.*

Michelle scrambled up. She raced around the barn, pulling Tom behind her. "I'm taking you into the woods," she told him. "You'll be safe there."

Michelle hurried along the bumpy dirt path that led to the woods. She had to keep tugging on Tom's rope. He wanted to stop and look at everything.

But when they reached the first row of trees, Tom darted ahead of her. Now Michelle had to run to keep up with the turkey!

Tom sped between two huge pine trees. *Whap! Whap! Whap!* The branches hit Michelle in the face as she raced after him.

"Slow down!" Michelle begged. But Tom moved faster—heading straight for a creek!

Michelle let go of the rope. Tom hopped right into the muddy water. He flapped his big brown wings. *Gobble, gobble, gobble.*

45

He sounds happy, Michelle thought. I bet he'll like living in the woods.

Michelle sat down on a mossy log and watched Tom take a drink. When he was finished, he waddled out of the creek and rubbed up against her legs.

Michelle patted him on the head and untied the rope around his neck. "I have to go back, Tom," she said. "And you have to stay here. You're going to live here now. You can't ever, ever go back to the farm, understand?"

Tom blinked his bright black eyes at her. Michelle stood up and emptied the corn out of her pockets.

"Good-bye, Tom," she said. "I'm going to miss you. You were the only animal on the whole farm that liked me!"

Tom started pecking at the corn. Michelle wanted to stay with him a little longer. But she knew someone might come looking for her—and find Tom.

Michelle turned and ran back to the Andersons' farm. Joey was pouring himself a cup of coffee when she quietly opened the kitchen door.

"It's almost dark," he said. "What have you been up to all afternoon? Did you find something fun to do?"

"Uh, yeah. I, um, played in the hayloft," she mumbled.

"Guess what I found—a checkerboard. I put it on the table. Do you want to play?" Joey asked her.

"Sure," Michelle said.

She took off her coat. Then she sat down and started setting up the game. Joey plopped down in the chair next to her. "So what should we play for?" he asked.

"You still owe me four ice cream sundaes, two movies, and six packs of bubble gum from the other times I beat you this month," Michelle reminded him.

"That's why I want to play. I need a

47

chance to win some of that stuff back!" Joey exclaimed. He helped her arrange the red and black disks on the board.

"I go first," Joey announced.

Gobble, gobble, gobble.

Michelle jumped up. Her chair crashed to the floor.

"What's the matter?" Joey asked. "It's only that fat old turkey."

Michelle hurried over to the kitchen door and swung it open.

Tom stared up at her with his shiny black eyes. *Gobble, gobble, gobble.*

Chapter
7

♥ That night Michelle couldn't fall asleep. Only two more days until Thanksgiving, she thought. What am I going to do?

Tom probably got lonely in the woods. And I bet he ran out of corn. He needs a place to live where someone will take care of him and play with him.

Michelle sat up and snapped her fingers. The petting zoo! It would be the perfect home for Tom!

Michelle knew the bus for the petting zoo stopped at the end of the driveway. She could figure out a way to sneak Tom on—but she knew her dad wouldn't let her take the bus alone.

Stephanie gave a little snore in the next bed. Stephanie! I bet Dad would give me permission to go to the petting zoo with Stephanie!

Michelle slid out of bed and padded over to Stephanie. "Steph. Wake up," she whispered. She didn't want D.J. to hear her. D.J. would definitely try to talk her out of this one.

Stephanie snored again. Michelle gave her a little poke. "Steph, I need you. Wake up!"

Stephanie opened her eyes. She rolled over on her side so she could look at Michelle. "What?" she mumbled.

"I need you to go to the petting zoo with me tomorrow," Michelle said.

"You woke me up to talk about the petting zoo?" Stephanie complained.

"I'm taking Tom there," Michelle explained.

"Who's Tom?" Stephanie asked.

"Shhh." Michelle put her finger to her lips. "Don't wake up D.J. Tom is Tom the turkey."

Stephanie sat up in bed. "Michelle, I know you're upset about the turkey. But we can't take it to the petting zoo. It doesn't belong to us," Stephanie told her.

"If we don't take him, the Andersons are going to cook him for Thanksgiving dinner! Please, Steph," Michelle begged.

Stephanie hesitated.

Say yes, Stephanie. You've got to say yes.

"Dad wouldn't—" Stephanie began.

Michelle tugged on Stephanie's quilt. "Puh-leeeze."

"You aren't going to let me go back to sleep until I say yes, are you?" Stephanie asked.

51

Michelle shook her head.

"Then I guess I have to go."

Michelle awoke just as the sun was rising. She had a lot to do to get ready for Big Turkey Escape Plan #2.

She dressed quickly and rushed downstairs. "First one up again!" Maria cried when Michelle bounced into the kitchen.

"Uh-huh," Michelle answered. "Um, I was wondering if you had a baby carriage or something like that. I brought one of my dolls with me and I wanted to wheel it around the farm."

Michelle was really too old to play with a doll carriage. But she hoped Maria didn't know that.

"I'm pretty sure there is one up in the attic. This house used to belong to my grandmother. She crammed all kinds of stuff up there. I'll take you up and you can explore, how's that?"

"Great! Thanks," Michelle said.

Maria led Michelle up to the attic. "Feel free to play with anything you find," she said. "I have to go down to the cellar and check our supplies. Just give a shout if you need me."

Michelle poked through the old clothes and furniture and boxes of pictures and letters. She found a huge stuffed panda almost as big as she was. It had on a pin that said OREGON STATE FAIR, 1949.

She found a rusty wagon—but she needed something with a top. Then she saw it—behind a dressmaker's dummy. A big, black baby carriage.

Michelle hauled it out to the middle of the attic. Yes! she thought. This will be perfect for my plan.

She struggled down the stairs with the carriage, then wheeled it out to the barn. She hoped no one would notice it behind Tom's pen.

"I'll be back in a little while," she promised Tom. She ruffled the feathers on his back. "I have a few more things to do before we can leave."

Michelle ran back into the house and upstairs to her room. She glanced over at Stephanie and D.J. Both still asleep. Good! They wouldn't like what I'm about to do.

Michelle pulled her long blue and white nightgown out of one of the dresser drawers. She held it up in front of her. This should work, she thought. I just have to cut slits in the sides.

Michelle quietly pulled D.J.'s little scissors out of her sister's makeup bag. It was hard to cut through the flannel material with the tiny scissors, but she managed to make a big hole on each side of the nightgown.

Okay, she thought. Next step. I have to ask Dad to let me go to the petting zoo. Michelle stuffed the nightgown in her backpack and raced downstairs to the kitchen.

Her dad stood at the stove with a spatula in his hand.

"Good morning," Danny called. "I'm making French toast, waffles, and pancakes. Which would you like?"

Maria returned from the cellar with a jug of apple cider and some maple syrup.

"Waffles. Dad, can I go to the petting zoo today? Stephanie said she would go with me," Michelle blurted out.

"Why would you want to go there? There are all kinds of animals right here," Danny said.

"You're welcome to pet any of them," Maria added. "Just check with Sam or me."

"Thanks," Michelle said slowly. "But I want to play with some animals that aren't farm animals. Remember what you told me about *farm* animals, Dad? You said a farm wasn't a petting zoo."

"I understand," Danny told her. "I don't see why you and Stephanie can't go."

"Great! I'll go wake her up!" Michelle tore up the stairs. The faster she could start her plan, the better.

She ran over to Stephanie's bed and shook her. "Time to get up! You promised we could go to the petting zoo!"

"Okay, okay," Stephanie muttered. But she didn't move.

"I'm not leaving until I see you standing up!" Michelle yanked on Stephanie's comforter.

"I said okay!" Stephanie climbed out of bed and stretched. "Happy now?" she asked.

"Yep." Michelle ran out the door and down the stairs. She barreled into the kitchen.

"Are you always so peppy in the morning?" Maria laughed.

"Sure!" she answered. "Dad, are my waffles ready?"

"All hot and toasty," he said. He set a

plate of walnut waffles down in front of her. Michelle ate them so fast, it made her stomach hurt.

"Slow down. You have half an hour before the bus comes," Maria said.

Stephanie shuffled into the kitchen and sat down. "We're leaving soon—so eat fast!" Michelle ordered. "I have to go outside for a minute."

She picked up her backpack and grabbed her jacket from the kitchen closet. She raced out the door before anyone could ask her where she was going.

Michelle ran straight to Tom's pen. "Almost time, Tom," she called. She opened her backpack and pulled out the nightgown. "We're going to play dress up," she told the turkey.

But when she tried to slip the nightgown over Tom's head, he went crazy. Gobbling, and flapping his wings, and scratching the ground with his claws.

"Tom, this is important," Michelle said firmly. "You have to let me put this on you. She planted a foot on each side of the turkey and held him still with her legs. He didn't like that one bit!

Michelle leaned down and forced the nightgown over his head. Then she slid his wings through the slits she made in the sides. Tom scurried to the other side of the pen the second Michelle let him go. The ruffled hem of the nightgown trailed behind him.

He still needs something else, Michelle thought. She chased Tom around the pen until she had him trapped in a corner. Then she tore the ruffle off the bottom of the nightgown. She tied the ruffle around Tom's head for a scarf.

Better, she thought. "Sorry, Tom," Michelle said. "But it's only for a little while, I promise."

Now she just had to get him into the carriage. Michelle didn't think she could lift the big turkey that high. She dashed to the corn bin and grabbed two handfuls of corn. She made a trail from the baby carriage to Tom.

He ate the kernels of corn—moving closer and closer to the carriage. "Look, Tom," Michelle called. She dumped the rest of the corn into the bottom of the carriage.

Tom hopped and flapped. Michelle gave him a little boost. And he was inside, happily eating the corn.

Michelle pulled the top of the carriage down as far as it would go. Then she wheeled Tom over to the kitchen door. "Steph! Let's go!" she yelled.

Stephanie came out the kitchen door with a piece of French toast in her hand. "He's in there?" she whispered, pointing to the carriage.

Michelle nodded.

"I can't believe I'm doing this," Stephanie grumbled as Michelle led the way down the driveway. A few minutes later the bus that stopped at the petting zoo arrived.

"What's in the carriage?" the bus driver asked.

"One of my dolls," Michelle said. Michelle and Stephanie each took an end of the carriage and hauled it onto the bus.

Gobble, gobble, gobble.

"Oh, no!" Michelle gasped. Tom's already out of corn.

"What was that?" the bus driver asked suspiciously.

"Umm, it was her stomach." Michelle pointed to Stephanie. "She didn't get to finish her breakfast."

Stephanie scowled.

The man nodded.

Michelle and Stephanie pushed the carriage to the back of the bus. They sat down on the seats next to it. The bus rolled down the road.

Gobble, gobble, gobble.

"That sounds like a turkey!" a young blonde woman a few rows ahead of them said. She held a doughnut covered with powdered sugar.

"That's great!" Michelle called back. "I'm practicing for my school's Thanksgiving pageant. I'm the Thanksgiving turkey. Gobble, gobble, gobble!"

"You're very good," the woman said. She took a big bite of her doughnut.

Tom stuck his head out of the carriage and gobbled back at Michelle. "Tom, get down!" Michelle whispered.

The turkey didn't listen. He flew out of the carriage and landed on the head of the man in the row ahead of him. The man jumped up and screamed.

"What's going on back there?" the bus driver yelled.

Michelle lunged toward Tom. She reached for him just as he hopped off the man's head—but she only managed to grab three

61

of his long tail feathers. They came right out in her hand!

Tom strutted toward the blond woman, his nightgown dragging behind him. He snatched the doughnut away from her!

"I knew I heard a turkey," the woman screeched. "Give me back that doughnut, you ugly bird!" Tom trotted down the aisle. The woman picked up another doughnut and threw it at him. It bopped him on the head, coating his feathers with powdered sugar.

Tom ate the doughnut in two bites and continued down the aisle, blinking at the other passengers with his bright black eyes. Michelle hurried after him. Maybe I can tackle Tom and stuff him back in the carriage, she thought.

Before Michelle could pounce, Tom flapped his wings and hopped onto the steering wheel. His long tail feathers brushed against the bus driver's face. The man sneezed and sneezed.

The bus swerved to the right, swerved to the left, then squealed to a halt. "Off!" the bus driver ordered. He sneezed again. "All three of you. Right now!"

Chapter
8

♥ Michelle and Stephanie climbed off the bus. They wheeled Tom home and snuck him back in the barn. Stephanie even helped Michelle take the baby buggy back to the attic.

"What am I going to do now?" Michelle asked as they headed downstairs.

"I don't think there is anything you can do," Stephanie answered. "I'm sorry your plan didn't work. But at least Tom got a fun bus ride—and two doughnuts."

Michelle tried to smile. She knew Steph

was trying to cheer her up. But it wasn't working.

Everyone else tried to cheer her up too. Sam gave her and Joey a tractor ride. Her whole family went apple picking. Maria showed her how to use an old-fashioned butter churn that belonged to Maria's great-great grandmother. Aunt Becky and the twins took her to visit a mama cat and her kittens in the hayloft.

But Michelle never stopped trying to figure out another way to help Tom. She hadn't come up with one idea by bedtime, so it was hard for her to fall asleep.

Two of her big turkey escape plans had failed! She needed a new one—and fast. Thanksgiving was the day after tomorrow!

Finally she drifted off to sleep. When she woke up the next morning, she still didn't have a new plan to save Tom!

D.J. and Stephanie were already out of bed, so Michelle dressed and headed downstairs. Everyone sat at the kitchen table having breakfast.

"Hey, sleepyhead," Joey called. "Sam and Maria were just telling us about a big dance tonight."

"It's going to be great!" Aunt Becky said. Michelle sat down next to her. "A real country dance at the local firehouse. Maria is lending me a square dance costume. One with all those poofy underskirts."

Michelle tried to smile. She didn't want to spoil her family's good time. But all she could think about was Tom. There had to be another way to save him. There had to be!

"You're going to have a wonderful time, Michelle," Maria told her. "There is going to be lots of food and prizes."

"Prizes?" D.J. asked. "What do you have to do to win one?"

"You don't have to do anything," Maria answered. "They sell raffle tickets at the door for a quarter. At the end of the night they call out numbers. If one of your tickets matches—you win a prize."

"What kind of prize?" Stephanie asked.

"Maybe a home-baked pie," Sam said. "Or a painting by a local artist. A free haircut . . . It could be anything!"

"Sounds like fun," Jesse said.

Hmmm. Tickets and prizes. That gives me an idea. A small smile spread across Michelle's face. *A big idea for Big Turkey Escape Plan #3.*

"So how do I look?" Jesse called as he came downstairs.

"Great!" Michelle answered. He wore a white cowboy shirt, a jeans vest, and black pants. *I hope my dad looks as good as Jesse,* she thought. *Otherwise Big Turkey Escape Plan #3 will be a big flop too.*

Michelle ran upstairs. She found her father combing his hair in front of the mirror.

He wore a plaid shirt with navy pants, and a black leather vest.

Yes! Michelle thought. He looks perfect!

She felt the pocket of her jeans skirt to make sure all the little cards were still there. They were.

Everything is ready, Michelle thought. Big Turkey Escape Plan #3 cannot fail!

"Come on, Dad," Michelle said. "We don't want to miss any of the dance." She grabbed his hand and pulled him down the stairs and out to the van.

On the way to the dance, everyone laughed and joked. Except Michelle. She was too busy going over her plan.

She decided she needed to earn ten dollars tonight. She had five dollars of her allowance money with her. And Michelle was sure she could buy a frozen turkey for fifteen dollars.

That meant she had to sell ten dances with her dad. He looked so cute tonight. Michelle didn't think it would be too hard to find ten women who would be willing to pay a dollar to dance with him.

Then Michelle's problems would be over! Tom's problems would be over! The Andersons could have the frozen turkey for Thanksgiving dinner and Tom could keep living on the farm.

This is my best plan yet, Michelle thought. This one will definitely work.

Danny parked the van in front of the firehouse and everyone piled out. Sam and Maria pulled up in the parking space next to them. They jumped out of their truck and led the way into the dance.

Whoa! Michelle thought when they all crowded inside. This is great! The firehouse was decorated with bales of hay and colored lanterns. Everyone was dressed in flouncy dresses and colorful shirts.

At the other end of the room, Michelle could see a small wooden platform. Four musicians stood on top. One played the fiddle, one played the drums, one played the piano. And one played a metal bucket with strings on it!

Joey took everyone's coats. Stephanie and D.J. headed toward some teenagers sitting near the stage. "I'm going to check out the desserts, okay?" Michelle asked.

"Go ahead," Danny said. "Let me know what looks good."

Michelle squeezed through all the people and sat down in a chair by the dessert table. She stared around the room, wondering which lady she should talk to first.

"Take your partner," the fiddle player called out.

The dancers made two big circles. Women on the inside. Men on the outside. Michelle saw Aunt Becky and Jesse join in.

The band started to play. More people joined the circles. Michelle noticed a pretty woman with long red hair standing near the coffeepot. She was tapping her toe to the music. I bet she would like to dance with Dad, Michelle thought.

Michelle hurried over to her. "Do you want to dance with that man over there wearing the cool black vest?" she asked. "He's my dad."

"What?" the woman exclaimed. But she smiled and her face got a little red.

"He's a great dancer," Michelle went on. "And for only one dollar, he'll dance with you."

The woman stared at Michelle. "I've never paid anyone to dance with me."

"Oh, no! I forgot to say it's for a good cause!" Michelle reached into her pocket and pulled out a cardboard ticket she had colored with a felt-tip pen. "I'm selling dances with my dad to earn money. I'm trying to save an endangered species."

Michelle knew turkeys weren't endangered. But Tom sure was!

"Oh, now I understand!" The woman

71

laughed. "Sure, why not? I'll buy a dance with your dad." The woman gave her a dollar and Michelle gave her a ticket.

"You don't have to give the ticket to him. You can keep it as a souvenir," Michelle said. "Wait right here. I'll send Dad over."

So far, so good, Michelle thought. She rushed over to Danny. The music stopped. She had to move fast or the next dance would start before she arranged everything.

"Hi, honey," Danny said when he saw her. "How about a dance with your father?"

"Sure," she replied. "But do you see that woman by the coffeepot over there." Michelle waved to the lady with the red hair. She waved back.

"She told me she thought you were cute. She really wants to dance with you," Michelle said.

Danny grinned. "Really? Do you mind if I ask her? I'll save a dance for you later."

"Go ahead," Michelle said. "Don't worry about me. I'm meeting lots of nice people."

Michelle watched her dad walk away. When the music started up again she wandered over to a woman in a yellow dress. "See that man in the black vest?" she asked. "Don't you think he's a good dancer?"

In less than half an hour Michelle made half the money she needed. Who should I ask next? she thought. She gazed around the room. Then she saw something awful!

Two ladies Michelle had sold tickets to were asking her dad to dance—at the same time.

Oh, no! Why didn't I think of that? I should have sold each dance separately, right before it started!

The two ladies and her father all turned to stare at Michelle. She tried to smile.

Danny headed across the dance floor toward her. "Michelle, we have to have a little talk," he said when he reached her.

Danny led Michelle out into the hallway. "Why are you charging women a dollar to dance with me?" he asked.

"I—I'm raising money for an endangered species," Michelle stuttered. She could feel her face growing hot.

"That's what those women said. *What* endangered species?"

"I wanted to buy the Andersons a frozen turkey," Michelle confessed. "I can't let them eat Tom. So I really was going to use the money to save an animal's life."

"I know you were. But you didn't tell me, and you didn't tell those women the truth. I want you to give them all their money back," Danny said.

"But if I do that, I won't be able to save Tom!" Michelle protested.

"I know you think you had a good reason for what you did," Danny answered. "But that doesn't make it right."

"I guess not," Michelle admitted. "I

should have asked you if I could sell the dances. I wasn't trying to trick those women—but I guess I did. I'll find them all and return their dollars, I promise."

Now what am I going to do? Michelle thought as she pushed her way through the crowded dance floor. Plan #3 was a total flop—and tomorrow is Thanksgiving.

Chapter
9

♥ "Don't you think Tom would make a great pet?" Michelle asked D.J. and Stephanie. They were up in their room, getting ready for bed.

"He's too big to keep in a cage," D.J. said. "And his gobbling would scare the neighbors."

Michelle knew D.J. was trying to make her laugh. But she couldn't. She felt too sad about Tom.

"Besides, you have Comet waiting for you back in San Francisco. He's your pet," Stephanie added.

"Yeah. I love Comet," Michelle said. "But I love Tom too. I want to at least say good-bye to him." Michelle grabbed her socks and shoes. "I'm going out to the barn."

"It's too late. You can't go out to the barn now," Stephanie said.

"I have to," Michelle argued.

"Go tomorrow morning," Stephanie told her.

"No, she should go tonight," D.J. said. "Tomorrow morning might be . . ."

D.J. didn't finish, but Michelle knew what she was going to say. Tomorrow might be too late.

"I'll be right back," Michelle promised. She hurried downstairs and grabbed her coat from the kitchen closet. She put it on over her nightgown and headed out to the barn.

Gobble, gobble, gobble.

He knows I'm here already. He's saying "hi," Michelle thought. "Hi, Tom," she answered as she walked to his pen. She opened the gate and stepped inside.

Tom trotted over and rubbed his soft chest feathers against her legs. Michelle crouched down so she could look right at the turkey.

"You're a great friend, Tom," she said softly. "I'm going to miss you so much. But I have to say good-bye now. I—I don't think we'll see each other ever again."

Michelle hugged the turkey. He didn't even try to squirm away. Then she stood up. "Bye," she whispered.

Michelle ran out of the barn. She couldn't stand to stay with Tom another minute. It hurt too much.

Gobble, gobble, gobble.

Tom's saying good-bye too, she thought.

The next morning Michelle dragged herself downstairs. I wish we could just skip Thanksgiving this year, she thought.

She found Maria and Aunt Becky and Danny and Stephanie and D.J. in the kitchen preparing for the big Thanksgiving meal.

"Good morning, honey," Danny said gently. "Did you sleep okay?" Michelle could tell he wasn't angry about the dance anymore—and that he was feeling bad for her.

Sam strode into the kitchen after Michelle. "I guess it's time for me to get that turkey," he said.

The kitchen grew quiet. Very quiet. Then everyone started talking in a rush.

Michelle raced out of the kitchen.

"Don't you want breakfast?" her father called after her.

"I'm not hungry!" she yelled.

She ran upstairs to the attic and curled up on a beat-up old sofa. She grabbed a pillow and pressed it over her head. "Oh, Tom," she moaned. "I'm sorry I couldn't save you! I tried so hard."

Chapter 10

♥ A little while later someone knocked on the attic door. Before Michelle could answer, the door opened. Her dad and Aunt Becky hurried inside.

"Where is the turkey, Michelle?" Danny asked.

Michelle jumped up from the sofa. "What?" she exclaimed.

"Sam went out to the turkey pen—and Tom wasn't there," he told her.

"Tom escaped. That's great!" Michelle felt so happy for Tom.

"It's not great," Aunt Becky said. "That turkey belonged to Sam and Maria."

"Did you set him loose?" her father asked, his voice serious.

"No!" Michelle cried. "I went out to the barn last night and said good-bye to Tom. He was in his pen then—and that's the last time I saw him. Really!"

Danny and Aunt Becky looked at each other. They don't believe me, Michelle thought.

"I—I did set Tom loose a few days ago," she admitted. "But he came back. Then I tried to take him to the petting zoo and I got kicked off the bus. I wanted to buy the Andersons a frozen turkey so they wouldn't have to eat Tom—but I couldn't earn the money."

Danny shook his head. "Go on back downstairs. I want you to stay in your room until it's time for dinner and think about why you owe Sam and Maria an apology. If you have anything to tell us about the turkey before then, we'll be in the kitchen.''

They still don't believe me! Michelle thought. But I didn't do anything with Tom last night. I didn't!

"Michelle, dinner!" Maria called.

Michelle didn't feel like eating. But it wasn't fair to spoil everyone's Thanksgiving, so she slowly headed downstairs.

Danny met her at the bottom of the stairs and led the way to the dining room. A lacy white tablecloth covered the long table. Candles and flowers decorated the center. All kinds of wonderful foods were set out, ready to be served.

Michelle knew there was something she had to do. "Sam and Maria," she said. "I have to tell you something." She glanced over at her dad and he nodded encouragingly. "I don't know where Tom is . . . but I did try and help him escape. It just didn't work. I'm sorry. I know Tom belongs to you. But I didn't want him to die!"

"I understand," Sam said. "It was hard for me when I first started working on a farm. I had to train myself not to get too close to the animals. I never give an animal that isn't a pet a name—that helps."

"Once the turkey became your friend Tom, I can see why you tried to help him," Maria added. "Let's have our Thanksgiving dinner," she said, changing the subject. "Michelle, would you go down to the cellar and bring up some apple cider?"

Stephanie jumped up. "I'll get it!" she exclaimed.

"No, I want to go," Michelle said. She was glad she told Sam and Maria the truth. And they were really cool about it.

Michelle rushed out of the dining room to the cellar door. She opened it and climbed down the narrow wooden steps. She spotted a big jug of cider on a shelf along the back wall and started toward it.

Thump!

Michelle froze. What was that? She peered around the cellar. She didn't see anything moving.

"I wish it weren't so dark down here," she muttered. She stepped around a couple of big cardboard boxes.

Thump!

Michelle spun around. That sound came from right behind her!

Thump! Thump!

One of the cardboard boxes jerked toward her.

"Helllp!" Michelle yelled. She scrambled across the cellar and back up the stairs. She ran into the dining room. "There's something in the cellar! Something alive!"

"What?" Danny exclaimed.

"I heard a thumping noise—and saw a box move by itself!"

"Sometimes a raccoon or a fox sneaks into the cellar and eats all the dried apples," Sam said. "Let's go down and find out what it is."

Sam led the way back down to the cellar. Michelle, Danny, and Jesse followed him.

"It was that box over there," Michelle explained. She stayed close to her dad.

Thump! The cardboard box bumped forward—straight toward Michelle!

Gobble, gobble, gobble.

"It's Tom!" Michelle yelled.

She ran over and opened the top of the big cardboard box.

Tom flapped his wings and hopped out. He rubbed up against Michelle's legs. Michelle gave him a big hug. She ruffled the soft feathers on his back.

Gobble, gobble, gobble.

"I missed you too, Tom," Michelle said.

"That's one lucky turkey," Sam said. He grinned at Michelle. "He made it through Thanksgiving without ending up on the table. And since he's such a good friend of Michelle's, I guess we'll have to make him one of the farm pets."

"Yes!" Michelle cried. She pumped her fist in the air.

They all trooped back upstairs and took their places around the table. "Well, we solved the mystery," Danny announced. "Michelle's friend Tom the turkey was in a box in the cellar."

"How do you think he managed that?" Jesse asked.

"You mean without someone helping him?" Danny said.

Stephanie jumped up. "May I be excused?"

D.J. leapt to her feet. "Me too!"

They started for the door.

"Steephaaanieee! DeeeJaaay! What's going on?" Danny asked.

Stephanie and D.J. turned back toward

the table. "You tell him," Stephanie whispered.

"We hid the turkey," D.J. admitted.

"We had to!" Stephanie cried. "Tom is Michelle's friend—we couldn't eat him!"

Before Danny could say a word, Michelle jumped in. "We forgot to go around the table and say what we're thankful for," she said. "I'm *thankful* to have such great sisters." Michelle grinned at Stephanie and D.J. "And to live with a whole house full of other great people. And I'm thankful that Maria and Sam invited us to the farm—"

Gobble, gobble, gobble.

Tom poked his head into the dining room. Everyone laughed.

"And I'm thankful for Tom—the best Thanksgiving turkey I *never* had!"